BEASTQUEST

❖ BOOK TEN ❖

VIPERO
THE SNAKE MAN

ADAM BLADE

ILLUSTRATED BY SCOTT DAWSON

SCHOLASTIC INC.

New York Toronto London Auckland Sydney
Mexico City New Delhi Hong Kong Buenos Aires

To Adam

With special thanks to Cherith Baldry

ISBN-13: 978-0-545-06866-6
ISBN-10: 0-545-06866-5

Beast Quest series created by Working Partners Ltd., London.
BEAST QUEST is a trademark of Working Partners Ltd.

Published by Scholastic Inc., 557 Broadway, New York, NY 10012, by arrangement with Working Partners Ltd.

12 11 10 9 8 7 6 5 4 3 2   9 10 11 12 13 14/0

Designed by Tim Hall
Printed in the U.S.A.
First printing, March 2009

Did you think it was over?

Did you think I would accept defeat and disappear?

No! That can never be. I am Malvel, the Dark Wizard, who strikes fear into the hearts of the people of Avantia. I still have much more to show this kingdom, and one boy in particular — Tom.

The young hero liberated the six Beasts of Avantia from my curse. But his fight is far from over. Let us see how he fares with a new Quest, one that will surely crush him and his companion, Elenna.

Avantia's Beasts had good hearts that I corrupted for my own wicked purpose. Now, thanks to Tom, they are free to protect the kingdom once more. But I have created new supreme Beasts whose hearts are evil and so cannot be set free. Each one guards a piece of the most precious relic of Avantia, which I have stolen: the suit of golden armor that gives magical strength to its rightful owner. I will stop at nothing to prevent Tom from collecting the complete suit and defeating me again. This time he will not win!

Malvel

THE SUN BLAZED DOWN OVER THE DESERT. Sand dunes stretched in all directions as far as the eye could see. There was no shelter from the merciless heat.

A nomad, wearing long robes the same color as the sand, was stumbling among the dunes. His thin face was burned by the sun and he screwed up his eyes against the glare. His throat was parched and his lips were cracked. "Water," he muttered. "I must find water."

At the foot of a dune he spotted a small plant with dark, thick leaves. Falling to his knees beside it, he tore it up by the roots and crushed the leaves against his mouth, hoping to extract precious drops of water.

But, with an exclamation of disgust, he tossed the plant aside. The leaves scarcely held enough water to wet his lips.

He almost wished he had never agreed to take part in this deadly challenge. But if he could succeed in crossing the desert, alone and with no food or water, he would win great honor for his tribe. Yet if he couldn't find water soon, he would die here, his bones scoured by the sand.

He rose to his feet and brushed the sand from his robes, determined to set one foot in front of the other. He clambered painfully up to the crest of the next dune.

When he reached the top, shock and relief made him stagger. In front of him at the bottom of the slope lay a shimmering blue lake. Trees shaded it, their broad leaves swaying gently.

"I'm saved! I'm saved!" The nomad staggered down the side of the dune, his feet sinking into the loose sand. "My tribe will be the greatest of all. . . ."

But as he drew closer to the foot of the dune, the shimmering water began to fade and the trees vanished into the glare of the sun. The nomad fell desperately to the ground, grabbing handfuls of sand, which trickled between his fingers. The beautiful lake had been a mirage. There was no water. Shattered by the sudden loss of hope, he buried his face in his hands and began to sob.

After a while he realized that his sobs were echoing. He looked up and noticed what he had missed before. Rocks emerged from the sand just behind him, and between them was a dark gap, leading back into the dune. A cave!

The nomad's hopes revived, he stumbled into the cave, muttering a prayer of thanks for shelter from the burning rays of the sun. He took deep breaths of the cool air, and felt eddies of it swirling around his ankles.

Then the grasp of the icy breeze tightened and the nomad realized that something was wrapping itself around him. Terror struck like a sudden blow. He tried to run, but the grip on his ankles tightened further and he fell flat on his face. He kicked out frantically, reaching down to wrench at whatever was gripping him, then froze.

Around his legs were the coils of a snake! But this was no ordinary snake. The tail itself was grotesquely huge, each of its scales bigger than the nomad's hand, and above it was a human torso, patterned with a raw, angry red and a sickly green. Unlike an ordinary, cold-blooded snake, its body sent out a huge wave of heat.

The nomad choked in terror as his gaze traveled upward and he saw that the snake had two heads.

Its four eyes stared at him, narrowing in sinister hatred, then the heads reared back.

"No!" the nomad yelled.

But the two heads swooped down on him and two sets of fangs buried themselves in his neck. He saw nothing more.

CHAPTER ONE

FAREWELL TO ERRINEL

Tom drew Storm to a halt a few miles beyond the village of Errinel. Turning in his saddle, he looked back.

"I wish we didn't have to leave," he said to Elenna, who sat behind him on the magnificent stallion. "It's the first time I've been able to visit my home since I set out on the Beast Quest."

"It's hard," Elenna agreed sympathetically. "I miss my parents, too."

"I don't know when I'll see my uncle and aunt again." Tom knew that until Avantia was safe from the Dark Wizard Malvel, his Quest must come first — even before his family. It was his

destiny to defeat the evil Beasts and collect every piece of the magical golden armor, which Malvel had stolen and scattered across the kingdom. He already had three pieces: the helmet, which gave him extra-keen sight; the chain mail, which bestowed strength of heart; and the breastplate, which made him physically strong. They were tucked safely in one of Storm's saddlebags, ready for when he next needed them.

It's a good thing they're magical, he thought now. *They hardly weigh anything at all!*

Fear churned in his stomach as he remembered how, after the defeat of Soltra the Stone Charmer, Malvel had appeared in a vision, warning him there would be a heavy price to pay if he completed this next stage of the Quest. Even so, he was determined to carry on. Malvel had kidnapped their friend and protector, Wizard Aduro, and only by seeing the Quest through to the end could he and Elenna hope to set him free. Aduro himself had told them so.

"Tom." Elenna shook his shoulder gently. "We have to go. Another evil Beast is waiting for us."

"I know." Energy flooded through Tom as he pledged himself once more to his Quest. He leaned forward to pat Storm on the neck. "Let's go, boy."

Standing beside the stallion, his ears pricked and his plumy tail waving, Silver the wolf let out an approving howl.

As Storm began to trot along the road, Tom could smell the pungent scent of herbs Aunt Maria had given him as a parting gift, which were stowed away in his pocket. "I wonder what the herbs are for," he said to Elenna now.

"Your aunt told us they cure all sorts of illnesses," Elenna reminded him. "Let's hope we don't need them."

"I'm sure they'll come in useful somehow," Tom said cheerfully.

The road led into the hills. Trees covered the slopes and a narrow stream followed the winding of the road. The sun told them they had been traveling for about an hour when they came to a crossroads.

"Which way?" Tom asked.

Elenna reached forward to take Wizard Aduro's enchanted map out of Storm's saddlebag. Unfolding it, she studied it for a moment. "It's telling us to go south," she said. "That road will take us to the desert."

Tom urged Storm on, while Silver bounded eagerly ahead. "Traveling in the desert will be tough," he said. "Worse than the jungle, even. The heat might finish us off before we get near the Beast."

"That's true," Elenna agreed. "Silver!" she called out to the wolf. "Come back here."

Silver raced back to her, his tongue lolling.

"You're tiring yourself out," Elenna scolded him. "Just slow down. You need to save your strength if you're going to cope with the desert."

Silver waved his tail as if he understood and loped alongside Storm as they continued south.

"Does the map show which part of the armor we're looking for this time?" Tom asked Elenna.

Elenna held out the map so that Tom could see. Twisting around in the saddle, he saw the glowing red path leading down to the vast expanse of desert in the southernmost part of the kingdom. In the middle of it, two pieces of golden leg armor lay glittering on top of a sand dune.

There was no sign of Malvel's Beast, but Tom couldn't suppress a shiver, thinking of it lurking behind a dune, ready to strike. What hideous shape would this new Beast take?

"It's a long way," Elenna said.

"The horseshoe fragment from Tagus will help." Tom glanced down at his shield to see the magical token he had won when he released Tagus the Night Horse from Malvel's evil spell. It gave them extra speed. With its help, they traveled quickly, and it wasn't yet midday when the road led down through the hills and out onto a plain. There were no streams or pools here, and the grass was parched and brown.

Tom felt the heat of the sun beating on his shoulders. His mouth was dry. Storm's head was drooping and Silver's tail trailed on the dusty ground.

"We shouldn't take Storm and Silver into the desert with us," Tom said to Elenna. "The heat will be worse there."

Elenna hesitated. "That's true; they'll find it hard to cope. But we can't just leave them!"

"I know. We'll have to find someone to look after them."

Storm shook his head and let out a whinny of protest while Silver raised his muzzle to the sky in a loud howl.

Tom had to smile in spite of his worry. "They don't want to stay behind."

"No, but you're right, Tom." Elenna sounded sad but determined. "We'll look for a safe place for them before we get to the desert."

Dust stung Tom's eyes as he peered ahead. They were drawing near to the edge of the desert; on the horizon the sky shimmered with heat. Then he spotted something rising up out of the plain. At first he thought it was an outcrop of rocks. Then he realized that its edges were too straight to be natural. He drew the golden helmet out of the saddlebag and put it on. As he did so, everything became clearer and he realized he was looking at a huddle of houses.

"Look! There's a town," he said to Elenna, pointing.

Elenna let out a sigh. "Shelter at last! I've never been so hot in my whole life."

Tom closed his eyes briefly, dreaming of shade and a long drink of cool water. "Let's head for it. Maybe the people there can help us." Carefully he took off the helmet and put it back in the saddlebag.

"They might even look after Storm and Silver," Elenna suggested.

"And maybe they can tell us something about the Beast," Tom added quietly as he turned Storm's head toward the distant buildings.

CHAPTER TWO

THIRST

STORM'S HOOVES ECHOED ON THE COBBLES AS
Tom and Elenna rode into the little town. A hot
breeze whirled sand down the street. The buildings
were made from blocks of reddish stone, as if the
town had grown up out of the desert. Every door
was closed and the shutters were fastened across
the windows.

The street came to an end in a deserted
marketplace. Tattered canvas awnings flapped on
the abandoned stalls. A few dried cabbage leaves
were blowing about in the breeze.

Even in the heat, Tom felt a chill of
apprehension. Something wasn't right. . . .

"The whole town's deserted," Elenna said, gripping Tom's waist. "Where is everybody?"

"I don't know." Tom turned in the saddle to take in all the houses that surrounded the square. "Do you think Malvel's Beast could have driven everyone away?"

He climbed off Storm, his limbs stiff and aching from the long ride. Elenna slid down after him. "We ought to look for water," she said. "Storm and Silver need to drink, and we'll have to take water into the desert with us."

Tom pointed to a stone trough at one side of the marketplace. It was shaded by a gnarled, leafless tree. "That must be where the townspeople water their animals."

He led Storm over. Silver trotted ahead and let out a disappointed whine as he looked over the edge of the trough. It was completely dry. The sides were furred with green and there were a few scraps of trash in the bottom.

"There's no water at all!" Elenna said.

Before Tom could reply he heard the sound of a door opening. A voice called, "Hey! You there!"

Tom turned. A woman was poking her head out of an open door. She wore a loose brown robe and a brown cloth wound around her head, so he could only see her eyes and nose.

"Are you mad, standing out there in the heat?" she asked. "It'll kill you if you don't get inside." She held the door open wider and beckoned. "Come on."

Tom led Storm into the little shade cast by the tree, and looped his reins around a branch. Silver slipped underneath the stallion's body and collapsed on the ground, his jaws gaping as he panted.

Elenna bent down to pat his head. "We won't be long, boy," she promised.

Tom and Elenna approached the woman in the doorway.

"Do you know where we can get water?" Tom asked her.

The woman stared at him. "Water? There isn't any water. The heat has dried up all our wells."

"But that's impossible!" Elenna exclaimed.

"I wish it were," the woman said. "But even here, on the edge of the desert, we've never known heat like this."

Malvel! Tom knew it. This had to be the work of the evil wizard.

"Are you coming in or not?" the woman asked. "I can't bear to see the two of you suffering in the heat."

She stood back to let Tom and Elenna into the cool shade of the house.

Inside, window shutters kept out most of the light and heat. Tom drew a deep breath of relief that they were protected from the glaring rays of the sun.

The woman led them through another door and into a small room. In the dim light, Tom made out four or five people lying on the ground. They seemed exhausted by the heat, and hardly looked up as Tom and Elenna went in. Only one raised a hand in greeting.

A boy was lying on a mattress at the far side of the room. He kept tossing and turning and letting out low moans of pain. His face was flushed with fever. Elenna crossed the room and stooped down beside him to lay a hand on his forehead.

On the ground in the middle of the group was a shallow bowl of water. A man got up, dipped a scrap of linen into the bowl, then put the scrap to his lips to suck the water out of it. Tom exchanged a glance with Elenna as she returned to his side. These people must be desperate if this was the only way they could make their water last.

"We've got to do something to help," Elenna murmured.

Tom knew his friend was right. But first, he had to ask a favor.

He put a hand on the woman's arm and drew her to one side. "My friend and I have to go into the desert," he explained quietly. "Can't you spare us *any* water?" He felt guilty for asking when these people had so little. But the only way to help them was to seek out Malvel's evil Beast and defeat it, although Tom knew he couldn't tell anyone here about his Quest.

The woman's expression hardened. "Do we look as if we have spare water to hand out to strangers?" she asked sharply. "I'm sorry, but I have to put my own family first."

"But we must —" Elenna began.

"My advice to you is to go home," the woman interrupted.

"We can't do that," Tom said.

Their raised voices had attracted the attention of the other people in the room. They struggled to their feet. Suddenly, Tom was surrounded by men and women with angry faces and accusing eyes. One of the men curled his hands into clenched fists.

They don't understand, Tom thought. *And I can't explain. What am I going to do?*

CHAPTER THREE

THE BARGAIN

ELENNA ELBOWED HER WAY THROUGH THE group and stood beside Tom, her head raised defiantly.

Tom searched desperately for the right words. He needed to calm the townspeople and convince them to let him have some water. But how could he do that when they needed water for themselves so desperately?

The sick boy was still tossing on his mattress, muttering in his fever.

"I know!" Elenna exclaimed suddenly. Turning to the woman who had let them in, she asked, "How would you like to trade?"

Instantly, Tom realized what Elenna meant. Aunt Maria's herbs! "Yes, we don't expect you to give us water for nothing," he added hastily.

"What have you got to trade?" the woman asked.

"We can help him," Tom explained, gesturing toward the sick boy. "We have herbs that will cure his fever. Will you give us a skin of water in exchange?"

"I'll give you everything I have if you can do that," the woman replied. Her voice shook as she added, "He's my son."

The people crowding around Tom and Elenna began to relax, though they still muttered doubtfully to one another.

Elenna pushed past them and went to kneel beside the boy. "Fetch me some hot water, please," she said, "and a mortar and pestle."

The woman immediately brought the mortar and pestle and set them down by Elenna's side.

Tom took out a handful of the dried herbs from his pocket and dropped them into the mortar. Then Elenna ground them into powder with the pestle.

"He's very ill," she muttered softly, so only Tom could hear. "It's lucky we came when we did."

"And it's also lucky you know about herbs," Tom said. He felt a stab of anger. "This is all the fault of the evil Beast. We have to stop it!"

By the time Elenna had finished pounding the herbs the woman had returned with a bowl of steaming water. Elenna mixed the herbs into it. Then she raised the sick boy's head and held the bowl so that he could drink the mixture in small sips. His mother looked on anxiously while Tom dipped a rag into the dish of water and bathed the boy's forehead.

Almost at once the boy stopped moaning and let out a sigh of exhaustion. His eyes closed, and his breathing became deep and even.

Elenna gently lowered his head to the mattress. "He's sleeping now." She handed the bowl to his mother. "Give him the rest of that when he wakes up."

"Thank you." The woman used her headcloth to wipe tears from her eyes. "He hasn't been so quiet in days. I'll fetch your water."

Tom and Elenna went to the door to wait for her. The other people settled down again, their glances more friendly now.

A few moments later, the woman came back carrying a leather skin of water and handed it to Tom. She held open the door, and the baking heat of the marketplace hit them once more.

"I'm sorry I was so unfriendly," she said. "We've always welcomed strangers. But we've never known heat like this before. Times are desperate. Is there anything else I can do for you, to make up for it?"

Elenna glanced over at Storm and Silver, still

waiting beneath the tree. "We could ask her to keep the animals for us," she whispered to Tom.

Tom shook his head. He knew there was nothing more the woman could do for them.

"No, thank you," he said to her. "You've already done enough. We'll be on our way now."

"Good luck, then." She raised her hand in farewell as Tom and Elenna made their way back to Storm and Silver.

"Why wouldn't you ask her?" Elenna asked. "We agreed we can't take Storm and Silver into the desert!"

"We'll have to." Tom's voice was shaking; he found it hard to control himself when he thought of what he had seen in this desolate town. "These people have *nothing*! We can't ask any more of them. Besides, I'd rather risk Storm and Silver's lives in the desert than leave them with strangers who have no water or food to give them."

Elenna nodded. "You're right. We need to stay together. But it's going to be hard."

Tom clenched his fists. "This is all Malvel's doing!"

Elenna nodded. "I wonder where the Beast is hiding," she said.

"I've no idea." Tom gazed out past the houses to where the dunes of the desert rolled endlessly toward the horizon. "But it won't be long before we find out."

→ Chapter Four ←

Into the Desert

Tom and Elenna both took a drink from the waterskin. Then Elenna cupped her hands and Tom poured water into them so that Storm and Silver could drink. Tom fastened the waterskin securely to Storm's saddle and put on his golden armor: the helmet, chain mail, and breastplate. Then, leading the stallion, he set out along the street that led toward the desert.

A wall of heat hit them in the face as they left the shade of the last houses and stepped into the desert. The bare skin on Tom's arms began to prickle and blister. He could even feel the hot sand through the soles of his boots. Fear stabbed through him.

How could they bear this heat and still be ready to fight a Beast?

"Cover up," he called to Elenna. "The sun will burn our skin as badly as a fire."

He pulled his tunic down to cover his arms, and trusted that the magical golden armor would protect the rest of him. Elenna was wearing a long piece of fabric as a scarf, which she wound around her own head, covering her mouth and nose until all Tom could see was the slits of her eyes.

Before they set foot in the desert, Tom pulled out the compass that his father, Taladon, had left for him with his uncle and aunt in Errinel many years ago, before he disappeared. Once more Tom read the words inscribed on the back of it: *For My Son*. He had the chain mail for strength of heart, but when he looked at the compass he felt close to his father, as if Taladon were beside him, giving him courage.

As he peered down at the compass the needle

swung wildly between Destiny and Danger. Clearly, it was too soon in this Quest to use it. Tucking it away in his pocket, Tom set his teeth with determination. There was no choice; he and Elenna had to go on. He checked his sword and hooked his shield over his arm; it bore the magical tokens from the good Beasts of Avantia he had freed in his first Quest: Ferno the Fire Dragon, Sepron the Sea Serpent, Cypher the Mountain Giant, Tagus the Night Horse, Tartok the Ice Beast, and Epos the Winged Flame. He knew they would come to his aid if he needed them.

Slowly they headed farther into the desert. Both animals had become very quiet. Storm plodded on determinedly, while Tom and Elenna walked beside him. Tom reached up to pat his neck. "You're doing fine, boy," he murmured. "Let's hope we'll be out of here soon."

Elenna looked down to where Silver padded along in Storm's shadow. "When this is over," she promised, "I'm going to give you the biggest bowl of water in all of Avantia."

Silver let out an approving howl.

As they trudged deeper into the sand dunes, they lost sight of the town behind them. All they had to guide them was the glowing red line on Wizard Aduro's enchanted map.

The sun started to go down, but it glared as fiercely as ever and an eerie whistling noise filled their ears.

"What's that?" Tom asked, sharing a startled glance with Elenna.

Slowly they both turned to look behind them. At first Tom could see nothing but the rolling sand dunes.

Then Elenna pointed upward. "Look!" she cried.

Tom saw that the sun was growing hazier, as if a thin curtain had been drawn across it, and the sky was turning a dirty yellow color.

"That's sand!" he exclaimed. "It's a sandstorm!"

Above them, sand was swirling in the sky, churning like a celestial whirlpool. As Tom stared upward, it took on a horribly familiar shape.

Malvel!

CHAPTER FIVE

SANDSTORM!

THE DARK WIZARD'S CRUEL LAUGHTER echoed across the sand dunes. "The hero of Avantia!" he taunted. "Not finding the desert so easy, are you?"

The swirling sand expanded until it covered half the sky, and, suddenly, Tom and Elenna could see Wizard Aduro, his hands tied behind him. He was bound to a chair, which dangled on ropes from a pole. Beneath him a pit of boiling tar bubbled and spattered. Tom stared in horror.

"No!" Elenna gasped, clapping her hands over her mouth.

"What have you done?" Tom yelled, drawing his sword.

A sneering smile crossed Malvel's face. "What I've done doesn't matter. It's what you're *going* to do. Every time you doubt yourself on your Quest, I'll lower your friend's chair farther into the pit. Whether Aduro survives will depend on *you*, Tom the Hero."

Even as he spoke, Tom felt a flicker of doubt. How could he be responsible for Wizard Aduro's life? It was hard enough trekking through the fiery desert, with an unknown evil Beast waiting for him.

Instantly, Aduro's chair jerked downward, while Malvel's mocking laughter resounded in Tom's ears. "You see? Better stay confident, Tom, or Aduro will die."

"No!" Tom's anger helped him thrust away his brief doubts and the chain mail gave him extra strength of heart. He would defeat the evil wizard!

"While there's blood in my veins," he vowed, "I'll save Aduro!"

"You're *not* going to win!" Elenna yelled defiantly.

"Keep thinking that." Malvel sneered.

The vision of the Dark Wizard's face broke up as the sand shifted and swirled, and they lost sight of the helpless Aduro. For a moment despair swept over him again, but Tom resolutely fought it back. He couldn't doubt himself! Not now, when so much depended on him and the success of his Quest.

He slid his sword back into its scabbard as the sand whipped around him, stinging his eyes. Soon he realized that the sky was completely blotted out and he couldn't see Elenna or their animal friends, even though he knew they were standing close by.

"Tom!" Elenna's voice rose over the whistling of the wind.

Blindly Tom stretched out a hand, and was

relieved to feel Elenna's fingers close around it. They clung together for a moment, buffeted by the wind. Then a powerful gust knocked them off their feet and they sprawled in the sand. Somewhere, Silver was howling.

Tom could feel sand piling on top of them. He tried to push it away, but it kept pouring over him, streaming into his eyes and his mouth until he couldn't breathe. His heart pounded and fear froze his limbs. He and Elenna were completely buried!

Is this how my Quest will end? he thought.

Then Tom remembered that his golden breastplate gave him special strength. Perhaps he would be able to free himself and Elenna! Flexing his muscles, Tom heaved at the sand. At first, nothing moved; it was like pushing against rock. But Tom didn't give up; he kept on pushing against the crushing weight of sand.

Suddenly, he felt it give way. He forced himself upward, sand cascading all around him. He managed to stand, then kicked his way out of the mountain of sand that had piled on top of him and Elenna.

His friend was struggling to get up. Tom reached down, grabbed her by the arms, and helped her to her feet. Elenna stood beside him, coughing and spitting out sand, and trying to wipe it from her eyes.

Tom blinked and looked around. Although the storm was dying down, the air was still full of drifting grains of sand, but the magical helmet helped him to see clearly. Storm was standing a short way off and came cantering up as soon as Tom called to him. Tom patted his neck, thankful that the stallion was safe.

But where was Silver? Tom couldn't see any sign of the wolf.

He shook Elenna by the shoulder. "Silver's missing!" he said.

CHAPTER SIX

THE TRACK OF THE BEAST

A NEW DUNE HAD FORMED. TOM AND ELENNA clambered up the side of it, their feet sinking into the sand at every step. From the top, with the help of the golden helmet, Tom could see a long way across the desert. But in that entire vast expanse, there was not one sign of Silver.

"Silver, where are you?" Elenna called out, panic in her voice. "Silver!"

A drawn-out whinny from Storm made them turn and look down at the stallion. Storm flicked his head three times in the same direction, then whinnied again. Tom stared at him, puzzled.

"He knows!" Elenna shouted. "Tom, Storm knows where Silver's buried!"

Together they skidded down the dune and fell to their knees, digging frantically. Tom plunged his hands into the sand, but could feel nothing except for burning heat.

Then his scrabbling fingers touched something soft. "He's here!" he gasped.

He and Elenna dug in the same spot. At last they uncovered the top of Silver's head, his gray-white fur matted with sand.

"Yes!" Elenna punched the air in excitement.

She and Tom scooped away more of the sand until they could drag the wolf out into the open.

His body was limp. Fear stabbed at Tom's heart.

Elenna bent over her friend, using her scarf to wipe sand from his eyes and around his jaws. Suddenly, Silver let out a huge sneeze. He blinked, and his tail began to wag slowly, beating on the sand.

"He's alive!" Elenna exclaimed, tears in her eyes. "He's going to be all right."

The wolf staggered to his paws and gave himself a shake, scattering sand in all directions.

Grinning with relief, Tom went back to his horse, unfastened the water skin, and gave both Silver and Storm a drink. Then he and Elenna took a few sips.

The skin was still over half full, but Tom didn't know how much farther they had to go. He fastened the stopper firmly. "It's time we were on our way," he said.

"Yes, but where?" Elenna asked, looking around.

The desert looked completely different after the sandstorm. All their tracks had been wiped out. Now Tom couldn't tell which direction they had come from or where they were supposed to go.

He fetched Wizard Aduro's map from Storm's saddlebag. The glowing red line still pointed into the desert, toward the picture of the golden leg armor, but that wasn't much use when they didn't know where they were starting from.

The sun was reappearing through the haze as the sand gradually settled. It was much lower now and Tom didn't want to spend the night in the desert with Malvel's Beast lurking. They had to make a decision quickly.

"I think we should head for the sun," Elenna said, pointing. "We know it sets in the west."

Tom consulted the map again. The picture of the leg armor was west of the town. Briefly he hesitated. If he made a wrong decision now, it could mean the end of all of them. Then he remembered Wizard Aduro, hanging helplessly over the pit of tar. Tom knew he couldn't afford to be uncertain. He had to be brave and strong, or the good wizard would die.

"Right," he said, folding the map and putting it back in the saddlebag. "Let's go."

Leading Storm, he chose a route that wound between the sand dunes, heading as directly as he could toward the sun. The desert still throbbed with heat, and the hot wind hissed like a snake, whirling sand around them.

Tom was sweating inside his armor. Grains of sand had worked their way under the metal and into his clothes, itching unbearably. But he was determined not to lose hope. He would find the Beast and defeat it, for the sake of Aduro — and all of Avantia.

They had not been trudging through the sand for long when, through the visor of his helmet, Tom spotted something ahead, disturbing the smooth surface of the desert. He quickened his pace until he stood over it. It was a wavy track, running into the distance as far as he could see.

"It's beautiful," Elenna said, crouching down to

admire the pattern in the sand. "What could have made it?"

Tom shook his head, puzzled. "It looks like the sort of track Sepron would make if he were slithering around in the sand, instead of swimming in the sea."

Elenna glanced up at him. "Sepron would never come into the desert."

"No," Tom agreed grimly. "But we know something else is here."

"Malvel's Beast?" Elenna glanced around warily. "You think this is its track?"

Tom nodded. "We should follow it."

Elenna rose to her feet again. "Yes. The sooner we meet the Beast, the better."

Tom led the way. The track wound through the dunes until he began to wonder if it would ever end. He watched and listened carefully in case the Beast should suddenly appear, but everything was silent.

Gradually, he noticed that the desert was changing. Instead of endless sand dunes, rocks poked up out of the ground here and there. A few scrawny plants grew in their shade, and now and again they passed a clump of spiny cactus, towering over their heads. The track wound between the clumps, heading for a jagged line of rocks not far away.

"I think we're getting close," Tom whispered.

Elenna halted, glancing around warily. "This place scares me," she whispered. "I think we should leave Storm and Silver here, and go on alone."

"Good idea," Tom replied. There was no point taking their animal friends into needless danger.

He guided Storm and Silver into the shade cast by a rock. Then he gave them both a drink, tied the waterskin to his belt, and beckoned to Elenna. "Come on."

They followed the track again, toward the line

of rocks. From time to time the wavy pattern disappeared as the ground became more rocky, but there was always enough sand for them to pick it up again.

At last Tom saw the track disappear between two rocks. He exchanged a glance with Elenna. His whole body was prickling with tension; he *knew* the Beast wasn't far away.

He dropped to his knees and then to his stomach. "I'm sure we're close now," he whispered to Elenna. "We *must* stay quiet and hidden." Awkward in his armor, he wriggled forward along the ground. Elenna followed him.

He edged his way to the rocks where the track disappeared, and peered down. In front of him the ground fell steeply into a valley and there, sprawled on the sand below, was Malvel's Beast. Tom couldn't keep back a gasp of horror, and exchanged a glance with Elenna.

A hot breeze sprang up, whipping the sand into tiny whirlwinds, and whispering a name into Tom's ear:

"Vipero . . ."

Malvel cackled, his laughter echoing between the rocks.

↣ CHAPTER SEVEN ↢

A FIERY ORDEAL

TOM STARED DOWN INTO THE VALLEY. SO THIS was the Beast! Vipero had the body of a snake, which lay on the sand in coils of red and green. But where the snake's head would have been was the muscular body of a man. Its neck was split into two, and each part carried the flat, wedge-shaped head of a snake. The two heads swayed, hissing angrily, their tiny bright eyes scanning the desert.

Tom suppressed a shudder. Then he spotted the golden leg armor in the middle of Vipero's coils. The swirling decoration on the metal glittered in the sunlight.

Though Tom was still a long way from the snake man, he could feel the waves of heat that were thrown out by his body. It was as if a wall of fire separated them from Vipero.

"That's why the desert is even hotter," Tom whispered to Elenna.

"And why all the wells have dried up," she agreed.

Tom fumbled in his pocket to find his father's compass. He pointed it toward Vipero. The needle swung quickly, pointing straight to Danger.

But whatever the danger, he would have to confront the Beast. And he had to be braver than ever now, because any doubt would send Aduro deeper into the pit of boiling tar.

Tom put the compass away and unsheathed his sword. Elenna put a hand on his arm. In spite of the heat, her face was drained of blood and her eyes were wide with fear.

"What are you doing?" she asked. "I can't let you walk straight into danger like this."

Tom forced himself to smile. "I'm going to circle around and surprise Vipero from behind."

Elenna managed to smile, too. "That's a great plan."

Cautiously they began crawling around the edge of the valley, keeping low and crouching for cover behind the rocks. More huge, spiny cacti were growing there, and Tom and Elenna had to force their way between the tightly packed plants. Tom bit his lip to stop himself from crying out as the cacti tore at him, and Elenna gasped as one long spine drove deep into her hand. She pressed the end of her scarf against the wound where blood was welling out.

They were closer to Vipero now. Peering through the cacti, Tom could see the heaped coils of the Beast. The two snake heads were turned away from

them: One scanned the horizon while the other kept its eyes fixed on the leg armor.

The clumps of cacti grew even more closely in this part of the desert. As Tom thrust his way between two of the fleshy stems he felt a tug on his belt. Looking around, he stared in horror to see that the water skin had caught on one of the vicious spines. There was a long tear in the leather and their precious water was leaking away into the sand.

"No!" Elenna cried. She grabbed the ruined water skin and put it to her lips, sucking up the last few drops of water.

Instantly, Tom heard a loud hissing from the valley where Vipero was lying. The two snake heads had whipped around, and the Beast's four eyes glared with a red light as he tried to see where the cry had come from.

"Get down!" Tom whispered.

He and Elenna lay flat. Tom's heart pounded and his muscles tensed. Gradually he relaxed; Vipero hadn't spotted them.

"I'm sorry," Elenna murmured.

"It's all right," Tom replied. Even so, he was asking himself how they could possibly defeat the Beast and get safely out of the desert, now that they had no water at all. His mouth already felt parched.

Once again he pulled his father's compass from his pocket and held it in Vipero's direction. At first the needle whirled about uncontrollably, refusing to settle. Then a faint shadow seemed to pass across the desert. Tom glanced up to see a small cloud drifting across the sun. When he looked at the compass again, the needle pointed toward Destiny.

"It's time," Tom said.

CHAPTER EIGHT

POISONED FANGS

Tom and Elenna crept down into the valley. Before they'd gone more than a few paces Tom spotted a dried-up watercourse, leading down toward Vipero.

"Let's go this way," he whispered to Elenna. "It'll help us hide from the Beast."

They could move more quickly in the gully because the steep sides hid them from the snake man's view. But they still crouched and trod cautiously, in case the rattle of loose stones alerted the Beast.

Halfway down, Tom peered above the level of the rocks to check how far they had to go. What he saw made him freeze. In the bottom of the valley stretched a shimmering lake of blue water.

"How did we miss seeing that?" he whispered to Elenna.

But his friend was already scrambling out of the gully and running down the slope toward the lake. Tom followed her. His whole body burned with fever as he imagined plunging into the cool water.

He tripped over a rock and fell, then stumbled to his feet and staggered the last few paces. A hissing filled his ears as he flung himself to the ground, where he could see waves lapping against the sand.

But instead of cool water, he felt only scorching sand. Tom let out a cry of pain and frustration. It was a mirage, an illusion. The floor of the valley was a fiery pit, not a lake. Beside him Elenna crouched with her hands covering her face, trying to hold back tears of exhaustion. Tom felt his throat tighten. In spite of the golden chain mail and the strength of heart it gave him, he knew he couldn't do any more; the burning heat of the desert had defeated him even before he fought the Beast.

Then he remembered Wizard Aduro, hanging over the pit of boiling tar. He would be closer to it now, because Tom's courage had faltered. Perhaps it was already too late, and the good wizard was dead.

No! Tom refused to give up hope. He struggled to his feet, determined to carry on.

Then a shadow fell over him. Tom looked up, expecting to see clouds covering the sun. But the sky was clear blue. Looking down again, he saw the shadow swaying from side to side. The top of it separated into two distinct outlines, rearing back . . .

Suddenly, Tom realized what he was looking at — the Beast's shadow! He leaped to one side just as Vipero's double fangs snapped on empty air. Two arcs of poison jetted out and fell harmlessly onto the sand.

Tom grabbed Elenna by the shoulder and dragged her to her feet. "We have to fight the Beast — now!" he yelled.

Vipero's two snake heads stabbed at Tom and Elenna, his fangs bared and his forked tongues flickering in and out as he hissed in defiance. Tom choked on the foul, acrid stench that came from his gaping jaws.

"That way!" he cried. As he dodged to one side, Elenna dove in the opposite direction, rolling in the sand and springing up again.

Vipero's heads hissed furiously. Tom realized how difficult this fight would be; the snake man was the first Beast they had faced who could attack both of them at the same time. He drew his sword and flung up his shield, just in time to ward off the

head that swooped down toward him. Vipero's fangs struck vainly at the polished surface.

"Elenna!" Tom called. "We have to distract him. When I give the signal, pounce on him from behind."

Elenna raised a hand to show she'd heard. She was panting in the hot, dry atmosphere, but she looked determined now.

Tom swung his sword, the blade slicing through the air just below Vipero's heads. The Beast hissed in anger. He reared back again, and Tom knew he was getting ready to strike.

"Now!" he yelled at Elenna.

Elenna threw herself forward, grabbing the snake man's tail. Startled, Vipero whipped around one head.

Tom wasn't prepared for how fast he was. Before he could do anything, the Beast's head struck down and Vipero sank his fangs into the soft flesh of Elenna's arm.

Elenna let out a scream of agony and lost her grip on Vipero's tail. For a moment she staggered on the sand. Then she slipped to the ground and lay there, motionless.

Tom stared in horror at the body of his friend. What had he done?

CHAPTER NINE

BATTLE AGAINST THE BEAST

TOM STOOD RIGID AS VIPERO TURNED TO FIX him with a hypnotic gaze. He couldn't believe what had happened. He wanted desperately to run to Elenna — but that was impossible while Vipero stood in the way.

"Come on, then, snake man!" he shouted, the golden chain mail giving him extra strength of heart. "Are you brave enough to face my sword?"

Vipero's two heads bobbed back and forth; Tom couldn't tell when they were going to strike. If he tried to concentrate on one of them, the other would dart forward, fangs bared. He slashed with his sword, but the heads swayed back out of range, and Vipero still blocked the way to the glittering leg armor and Elenna.

Sweat was pouring off Tom's body. His head swam with the heat. He knew he couldn't go on fighting for much longer. Vipero would weaken him and then strike when he was defenseless. Now that he was alone, he couldn't hope to defeat a Beast with *two* pairs of eyes watching him closely and *two* heads that could attack him separately.

Suddenly, Tom heard the sound of galloping hooves. At first he thought he must be imagining it, but glancing over his shoulder he saw Storm and Silver racing down into the valley. Tom felt a new surge of energy as he realized that his animal friends had come to help.

Storm's coat was slick with sweat and Silver was panting rapidly, but they ran straight up to Vipero without hesitating. Turning away from Tom, the Beast loomed over the stallion and the wolf, his jaws gaping as if he were going to eat them alive.

But Storm and Silver stood firm. Silver let out a ferocious howl while Storm reared up and pawed at the air with his hooves.

Now Tom saw his chance. He charged forward and slashed at Vipero. His blade sliced easily through the Beast's necks, severing both heads with one blow.

The Beast's body fell to the ground with a dull thud. The snaky coils twitched once or twice and then were still.

Tom sagged with relief. Another of Malvel's evil Beasts had been defeated! Now he would be able to help Elenna.

But before he could move, Tom heard a vicious hissing. The two snake heads were moving! For a moment Tom could do nothing but gaze at them in horror. The rest of Vipero's body lay still, but the heads had a life of their own!

Tom could never have known that this was going to happen. *I need more help*, he thought. He looked at the magical tokens embedded in his shield. Which of Avantia's friendly Beasts could he call upon?

"Epos!" he said aloud, and frantically rubbed the phoenix feather in his shield, imagining the great flame bird instantly swooping to his rescue. But though he searched the sky with the help of his golden helmet, he couldn't see anything. There was no sign of the friendly Beast.

Suddenly, the two snake heads darted toward Tom. Desperately, Tom slashed at them with his sword.

"Epos, where are you?"

He swung his shield, trying to ward off both heads at once as they bared their fangs again, ready to strike. But the weight of the shield threw Tom off balance. He fell sprawling onto the hot sand, and lost his grip on his sword.

It's over, he thought. *Malvel has won.*

CHAPTER TEN

EPOS

JUST THEN, A HARSH SQUAWK SOUNDED ACROSS the valley. He rolled over and looked up.

It was Epos!

The magnificent phoenix blazed across the sky. Her red-gold wings shone brighter than the sun. Fire streamed from her tail and golden light flashed from her claws. She swooped down, her talons stretched out toward Vipero's two snake heads, which flinched away from the shining claws.

Epos soared upward again, but as Vipero's heads slithered back toward Tom, the Winged Flame swooped down, forcing them away. The heads darted back and forth with a menacing hiss, but at every turn the noble Beast barred their way.

Tom sprang to his feet. Looking around, he spotted his sword lying at the foot of a rock. He grabbed it and turned to face Vipero.

But he quickly realized that the heads couldn't be killed by the sword. If he slashed them in two, the remaining part would still attack. What could he do? Exhausted by the heat, he had to force himself to think of a plan.

Then he noticed one of the huge cacti nearby, its lethal spines poking out. That was it! If Tom could pin Vipero's heads to the cactus, he could destroy them.

Tom backed toward the plant, waving his sword at the two heads. "Come on!" he yelled.

Epos beat her flaming wings and hovered just above Tom. The two snake heads slithered rapidly across the sand and reared up, ready to attack.

Tom gazed up into the two sets of gaping jaws. The flesh of their throats was black, and their fangs were a rancid yellow, dripping poison that hissed on the sand. Tom choked as its acrid scent wafted over him once again.

One of the heads lunged forward with a furious hiss. Tom swiveled out of the way just in time. Moving too quickly to change direction, the head sank its fangs right into the cactus. It tugged back, but, trapped by the spines, it couldn't move.

"Stuck!" Tom yelled in triumph.

He plunged his sword into the thick flesh of the Beast, pinning it to the cactus. Silver blood, like a river of mercury, poured from the wound.

Meanwhile, Epos had swooped down on the second head and slammed it against the cactus with her talons. Pulling away, she left one golden talon in place, pinning the head beside its companion.

Epos soared into the air again. Beating her wings together, she gathered a ball of fire and launched it toward the cactus. When she had been cursed by Malvel's evil spell, Tom had been her target. Now she was creating her fearsome fireballs to help him.

Vipero's two heads writhed, trying to free themselves. Tom pulled out his sword and stepped back to avoid the fireball. But as the blazing sphere hurtled through the air, trailing flame behind it, he saw that it was going to miss Vipero. Raising his shield, he batted the fireball so that it landed on target. The fireball exploded on impact, engulfing the Beast.

The outlines of the snake heads began to shimmer in the heat. An eerie shriek rose up to the sky, then stopped abruptly. The two snake heads disappeared. In their place, hundreds of tiny bright green snakes erupted from the fire and slithered away into the desert. They headed for gaps among the rocks or burrowed down into the sand. Within moments, they were gone.

Tom let out a long sigh of relief. Vipero was defeated. "Thank you, Epos!" he called.

But there was no time to celebrate his victory. He had to think of Elenna. Tom ran across the sand to his friend and flung himself down beside her. Silver was standing over her, whining anxiously.

Elenna was still unconscious, but her chest was rising and falling as she breathed. Her arm was red and swollen where Vipero had pierced it with his fangs.

As quickly as he could, Tom pulled the remains of Aunt Maria's herbs out of his pocket. He held Elenna's head in his lap and rubbed leaves into the snakebite. Elenna still didn't move.

Tom tore up a leaf and dropped the pieces into

his friend's mouth. "Elenna, you've got to swallow them!" he begged her.

Epos hovered above. A single crystal tear fell from her eye and dropped into Elenna's mouth. Elenna stirred, licked her lips, and swallowed the herbs.

Silver lowered his head and nudged Elenna's shoulder gently. Her eyes fluttered open. She looked at Tom, and then at Epos. A smile spread over her face.

"Tom, you won!" she exclaimed.

Tom helped her to sit up, and Silver covered her face with licks. Elenna plunged her hands into the wolf's thick fur and hugged him. Already Tom could see that the swelling on her arm was going down and the red streaks were fading.

Tom's limbs were shaking with exhaustion. Just then he spotted the two pieces of golden leg armor glinting nearby. He pulled them on and, as he did so, his exhaustion vanished and he felt as if he could run forever. He had won another new strength!

He gazed around at the sand dunes stretching into the distance on every side. Even if he could run forever, how were they all going to get out of here? The intense heat of the desert was fading now that the Beast was dead. But it was still too hot to travel easily, and the last of their water was gone.

Then Epos let out a squawk, and landed softly on the sand.

"I think she's offering us a lift!" cried Tom.

Elenna scrambled up onto the flame bird's back, and Silver leaped up after her. Tom even managed to lead Storm onto the back of the enormous bird.

When the friends were settled, Epos beat her wings and took to the air again. The sun was starting to set, covering the vivid blue sky with

ribbons of scarlet. The dunes of the desert sped smoothly beneath them as they flew.

Then Tom spotted a small, dark cloud scudding toward them. As it drew closer he saw it take on the shape of Malvel. Wizard Aduro, still bound in the chair, was dangling lower than ever over the pit of boiling tar.

Anger surged through Tom; he gripped Epos's neck feathers. "I kept my courage and I defeated Vipero!" he shouted.

Malvel's deep-set eyes glittered menacingly. Tom could tell that he was furious to see Tom and Elenna emerging alive from the desert.

"You may have won this time," he sneered, "but the next Beast will be the real test. I'd like to see you escape from that!" He let out a peal of cruel laughter. "You've never seen a spider like it!"

"I'll fight any Beast you send against me!" Tom retorted.

"Why don't you fight us yourself?" Elenna taunted the evil wizard. "Or are you too much of a coward?"

There was no reply. The vision of Malvel and Aduro faded as the dark cloud thinned and disappeared. Epos spiraled gently downward and landed on the edge of the desert, near the town.

Tom, Elenna, Silver, and Storm scrambled to the ground. At once the mighty bird took off again, her blazing wings carrying her high into the sky.

"Thanks!" Tom called out. "I hope we meet again!"

Elenna raised a hand to wave good-bye.

Epos circled once above their heads and flew away, growing smaller and smaller until she was a tiny, red-gold spark. Then she was lost to sight in the blaze of the setting sun.

The friends stood quietly for a moment.

Then Elenna smiled. "You look like a true knight now."

Tom drew himself up. Wearing the golden helmet, chain mail, breastplate, and leg armor, he *was* beginning to feel like a knight.

But would that be enough? Tom knew there would be another test as he faced the next Beast. Would he be able to defeat it? And would his heart be strong enough to keep Wizard Aduro alive?

Taking a deep breath, he summoned all his courage. "Come on, Elenna," he said. "We have a Beast to track down."